Peter Eldin

Fun and games with paper

diagrams by Phil Emms
cover photograph by Pete Smith

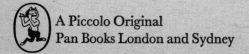
A Piccolo Original
Pan Books London and Sydney

First published 1976 by Pan Books Ltd,
Cavaye Place, London SW10 9PG
2nd Printing 1976
© Peter Eldin 1976
ISBN 0 330 24626 7
Made and printed in Great Britain by
Richard Clay (The Chaucer Press) Ltd, Bungay, Suffolk

Contents

1 Folding, cutting and drawing

Making it square

For many of the folds, tricks, and puzzles described in this book you will need a square piece of paper. If you only have a sheet of oblong-shaped paper this is how you can make it into a square: Fold the top right-hand corner diagonally to the left as shown in **figures 1** and **2**. Now cut off the piece at the bottom and you have a square piece of paper, **figures 3** and **4**.

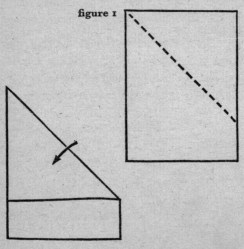

figure 1

figure 2

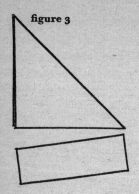

figure 3

figure 4

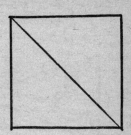

Sailor's hat

To make a sailor's hat for yourself you will need a sheet of paper the size of a newspaper – in fact a page from a newspaper will do very well.

Fold the paper in half as shown in **figure 5**. Next fold it in half again and then open it out so that you have made a crease down the centre. Fold the top corners over to meet the centre crease as shown in **figure 6**.

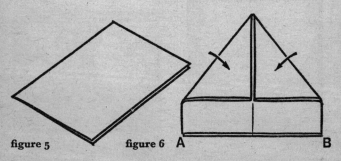

figure 5

figure 6 A   B

Fold the bottom section, A–B, upwards, turn the paper over and do the same with section C–D, as shown in **figure 6a**. Now simply place your hand into the opening at the bottom, open it out slightly, and your sailor's hat is complete.

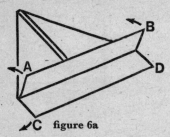

figure 6a

Fit for royalty

To make a crown fit for a king or a queen all you need is a piece of paper or thin card about 12 cm wide and long enough to go around your head.

Fold the paper in half and then in half again or, alternatively, you can fold it concertina fashion. Now draw one of the designs shown in **figures 7** and **7a** on

figure 7

figure 7a

to the top fold. With a pair of scissors cut along the lines you have drawn.

Open out the paper, join the two ends with glue or paper-clips into a circle and you have a crown fit for royalty, **figure 7b**. If you want to make it look even more regal, paint it in silver or gold and then cut out some coloured paper shapes and stick them on, to represent jewels.

figure 7b

figure 7c

Hat/cup fold

This is a very easy fold that produces a cup or a hat, depending upon the size that you make it.

Take a square sheet of paper and fold it in half diagonally, **figures 8** and **9**. Now fold the bottom right-hand corner to half-way along the opposite side,

figure 8

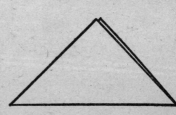

figure 9

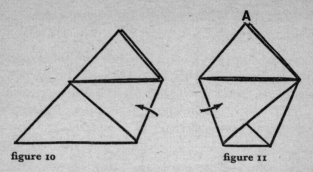

figure 10   figure 11

as in **figure 10**. Do the same with the bottom left-hand corner and your paper should look like **figure 11**. Bend the top corners, marked A in **figure 11**, one towards you and one away from you.

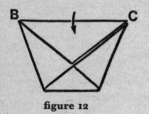

figure 12

Your paper should now be like that shown in **figure 12**. If you now open out the shape along the line B–C you have a perfectly good paper cup or hat. You could even use it as a paper boat.

A simple swan

To make this swan you will need a square sheet of paper.
Fold the paper in half diagonally to make a definite

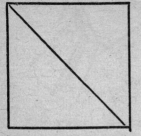

figure 13

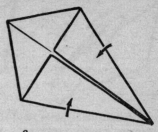

figure 14

crease from corner to corner, and then open it out again as in **figure 13**. Now fold the bottom and the right-hand edges to meet the centre crease (**figure 14**) and fold the edges over to the centre once again (**figure 15**).

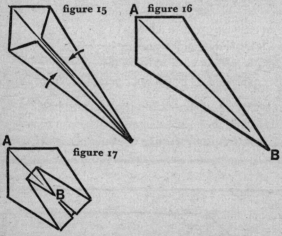

figure 15　　A　figure 16

A　　figure 17

B

Turn the paper over and fold the point B (**figure 16**) up to touch point A, then fold it back a little as shown in **figure 17**. Next fold the paper in half along the line A–B, along the line of the original diagonal crease mark. When you have done this, pull up the neck and head of

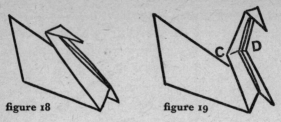

figure 18   figure 19

the swan as in **figure 18**. Pinch the base of the neck (place your fingers on C and D in **figure 19** to do this) and this will keep the neck in an almost upright position, and your swan is finished.

Love-knot letter

This is an easy way to fold a letter to put through someone's letter-box or for posting in your school post-box. By folding your letter in this way you will not need an envelope and it will not open of its own accord.

Having written your letter fold the paper in half lengthways and then in half again so that you have a long, narrow strip as in **figure 20**. Fold along the dotted

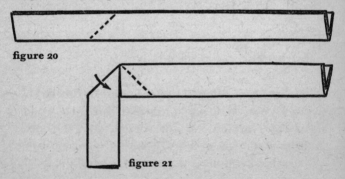

figure 20

figure 21

line in **figure 20**, so that the paper now looks like
figure 21. Fold backwards on the dotted line in **figure 21** and your paper will now resemble **figure 22**, with the right-hand tail longer than the other.

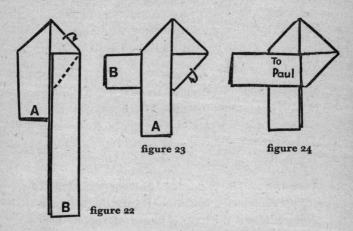

figure 23

figure 24

figure 22

Fold backwards along the dotted line in **figure 22**.
Now take tail A (**figure 23**), tuck it behind tail B, and your love-knot letter is complete, **figure 24**. All you now have to do is to write the person's name on the front.

Using tracing paper

Tracing paper is a very useful thing to have about the house if you like drawing or if you would like to copy pictures, maps, or diagrams from books and magazines. It can be bought in sheets from your local stationer.

This is how you use tracing paper to make an accurate copy of something:

Place the tracing paper over the picture to be copied. If you can stick the tracing paper down without damaging the book from which you are copying, then do so; for it is important that the tracing paper does not move. If you cannot stick it down, then you must make sure that you hold it steady.

With a pencil, draw on the tracing paper, following the lines of the picture beneath. When you have finished you will have a copy of the picture on the tracing paper. This can be transferred on to a sheet of ordinary paper, as follows:

Turn the tracing paper over and cover the back of your copy with pencil as shown in **figure 25**. Whilst you are doing this, rest the tracing paper on a spare sheet of paper that you do not want to keep, as the picture will come out backwards on this paper.

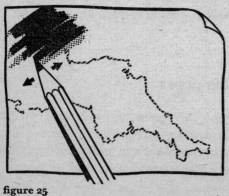

figure 25

Next, take the sheet of paper on which you wish the final drawing to appear. Turn the tracing paper over once again and, with a pencil (making sure that the tracing paper is held steady) go over the lines of your drawing. This will transfer an image of the drawing on to the sheet of paper underneath the tracing paper. Remove the tracing paper and then, with pencil, ink, coloured crayons or paints, complete the picture on the paper.

Drawing it larger

If you would like to copy a drawing or a map but would like it to be either larger or smaller, here is how to do it.

Copy the picture on to a sheet of tracing paper (see page 14). Now draw a square around the outside of the traced drawing. On the lines of this square make a mark every centimetre and then join them up with pencil lines to form a grid pattern as in **figure 26**.

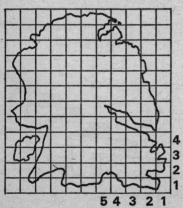

figure 26

On another sheet draw a similar grid but make the squares larger, as in **figure 26a**. If you want your picture to be smaller than the original then make the

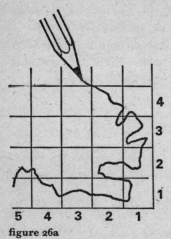

figure 26a

squares of the grid smaller. Now copy the drawing square by square, using the lines of the grid as a guide. Next, either carefully erase the lines of the second grid or, alternatively, trace the new picture and transfer it to a new sheet of paper as explained on page 14.

Hand in hand

To make a string of figures holding hands, you will need a long strip of paper. Pleat the paper, concertina fashion, as in **figure 27**.

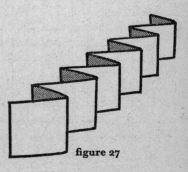

figure 27

Next, draw on the top fold the figure you wish to have, but make sure that at some point it touches each side of the paper or you will end up with several separate figures instead of one long row. The easiest way to make these joins is to draw your figures with their arms outstretched as in the example shown in **figure 28**. Cut round the lines and then open out the paper and you will have your row of figures, as in **figure 28a**.

figure 28

figure 28a

If you want to use this as a party decoration to be pinned on the wall, then it is a good idea to draw figures appropriate to the theme of the party. For example, if it is a Christmas party, you could make a string of angels; for New Year parties draw Old Father Time; for Hallowe'en parties make the figures look like witches; and so on.

When you have made your string of figures you can paint them to make them more decorative and, by gluing several lengths together, really long chains can be made to decorate the room.

The pattern maker

To draw a beautiful design like that shown in **figure 29**, all you need is a drawing-pin, a piece of card, a pencil, some paper, and a lot of patience.

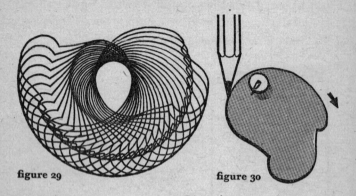

figure 29

figure 30

Draw a simple shape on the sheet of card and then cut it out. Pin the card to a sheet of paper and draw around the shape with a pencil. Move the shape a little and draw around it again. Keep repeating this action until you are thoroughly fed up and you will have a picture that looks extremely effective. **Figure 30** shows the shape used to produce the pattern in **figure 29**.

If you have infinite patience, use coloured pencils, using a different colour each time you draw round the shape. There is no need to complete a circle when drawing your design. Stopping half-way around can be just as effective. You could also make attractive patterns by combining several shapes in one design.

Frilly circles

Cut out a circle of paper. Fold it in half and then in half again. Now make a number of cuts, close together as shown in **figure 31**. When the circle is opened out it has an attractive fringe (**figure 32**).

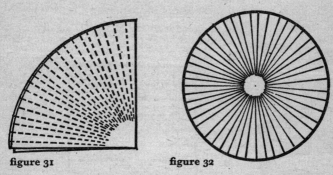

figure 31   figure 32

Frilly circles like this can be used as a decoration for a paper hat or strung together as in **figure 33** to make an attractive decoration. Affixed to a rolled-up sheet of paper as in **figure 34**, the frilly circle can be made into a pretty flower.

figure 33

figure 34

Paper sculpture

Many interesting shapes can be made out of paper quite simply by cutting, folding, and gluing. The unusual structure shown in **figure 35**, is, for example, made quite easily, as follows.

Take a rectangular sheet of paper and cut strips 2 cm apart, to within 2 cm of the centre, as shown in **figure 36**.

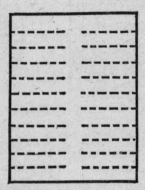

figure 35   **figure 36**

Take the two bottom strips and glue the ends together so that they form a loop in front of the sheet of paper. Do the same with each alternate strip. The remaining strips are glued together in the opposite direction until the sculpture is complete.

To make your sculpture a little different, why not try folding the strips so that they form squares rather than loops? Or, instead of gluing a left-hand strip to its opposite number, why not join it to the next strip above and see what sort of shape you produce? If you experiment with paper in this manner you will be pleasantly surprised at the number of variations that you can make from your cut strips.

Tearing a ship's wheel

For this you will need a double-page spread from a newspaper. Hold it with the newspaper's creased edge at the top, then (**figure 37**), fold this in half, as shown by the dotted line in **figure 37**. Next, fold the corner

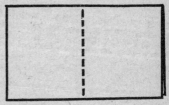

figure 37

marked A in **figure 38** to the position D. Then fold the edge BD to meet the edge BC so that you should now have the shape shown in **figure 39**.

Next thing to do is to cut or tear away the areas that have been shaded in **figure 39**. It is suggested that to

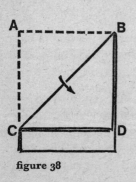

figure 38

figure 39

start with you draw the shape on to the paper with a pencil and then tear along the pencilled lines. After a while you will find that you no longer need these guide-

figure 40

lines and that they can be dispensed with. When you have finished tearing, open out the paper and you will have a magnificent ship's wheel, **figure 40**.

The fortune teller

Most people would like to know what is going to happen in the future. With this clever device you can pretend that you are able to tell fortunes.

Take a square piece of paper, fold it in half, then into quarters, and then open it out flat once again. It will now look like **figure 41**. Next, fold the four corners into the centre (**figure 42**).

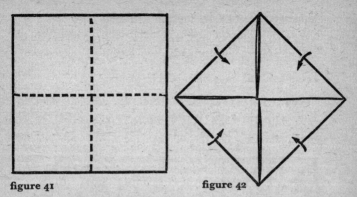

figure 41

figure 42

Turn the whole sheet over and write the fortunes on the corners as shown in **figure 43**.

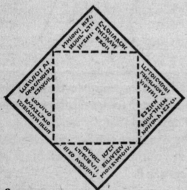

figure 43

Here are eight phrases that you can write on your fortune teller – or you may prefer to make up your own.

You will travel a great deal.

Riches and fame will be yours.

Good health will bless your life.

A letter containing good news is on its way.

You are about to receive some money.

You will marry young.

You will have two children.

Long life and happiness will be yours.

Fold the four corners into the centre along the dotted lines in **figure 43**. Write numbers on the flaps as shown in **figure 44**.

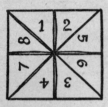

figure 44

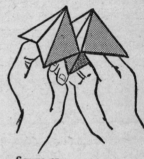

figure 45

Fold the square into half with the numbers inside. Then place each forefinger and thumb under the flaps as shown in **figure 45**. You will now find that, by moving your fingers and thumbs, you can open the fortune teller two ways – one way shows the numbers 1 to 4, and the other way reveals the numbers 5 to 8.

Hold the fortune teller open at 1 to 4 and ask a friend to choose any number. You then open and close the flaps for the chosen number of times. Ask your friend to choose any number he can see and again open and close the flaps the required number of times. For the third time ask him to choose a number. Lift up the flap bearing the selected number and read his fortune written under the flap.

Paper ladder

To make a paper ladder you will need a sheet of
newspaper, rolled up tightly like a roll of wall-paper.
Place an elastic band or a piece of adhesive tape on each
end to prevent the tube from unrolling. Now, with a
pair of scissors, make two cuts in the paper as shown in
figure 46. Be careful that you do not cut too far; about
half-way through is the correct distance.

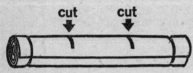

figure 46

Next cut along the top of the paper between the two
cuts. The position at this stage can be seen in **figure 47**.

figure 47

Fold the two outer pieces so that the paper now looks
like **figure 48**.

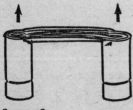

figure 48

Holding the two lower ends in one hand, use the other hand to pull the paper out of the rolls at the points indicated by the arrows in **figure 48** (this must be done very carefully or you will tear the paper) and you have a fireman's ladder (**figure 49**) – but do not try to climb it!

By making the original roll from a longer piece of paper, or two or more sheets of newspaper stuck together at their edges, much longer ladders can be made but the cutting is more difficult because of the thickness of the roll.

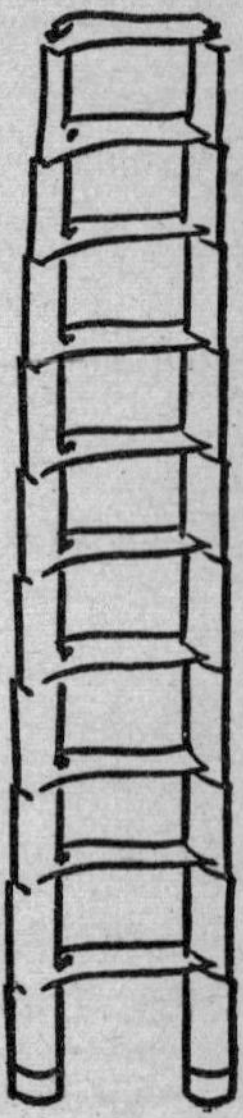

figure 49

Ladder in one

Here is a novel way of making the shape of a ladder in paper that requires only one cut of the scissors. Take a rectangular sheet of paper and fold it in half lengthways as in **figure 50**. Next fold the strip backwards and forwards, concertina fashion, as shown in **figure 51**, and

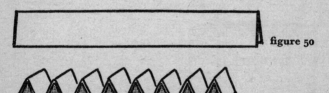

figure 50

figure 51

squash all the folds together, **figure 52**. Fold the packet in half as in **figure 53**, and cut along the dotted line as

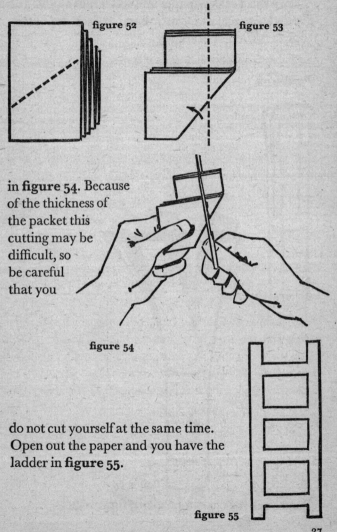

figure 52   figure 53

in **figure 54**. Because of the thickness of the packet this cutting may be difficult, so be careful that you

figure 54

do not cut yourself at the same time. Open out the paper and you have the ladder in **figure 55**.

figure 55

Paper tree

Take a sheet of newspaper and roll it into a tube. It is a
good idea to place an elastic band at each end of the
tube to prevent it unrolling.

Make four or five cuts in one end of the tube as in
figure 56.

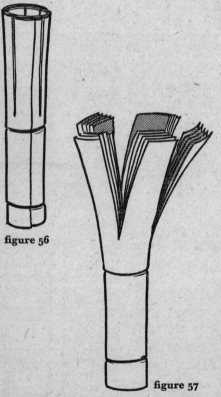

figure 56

figure 57

Bend back the cut-out portions, **figure 57**,

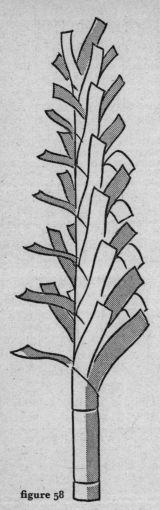

then insert one finger into the cut end of the tube and pull it out from the centre until you have a fully-fledged tree like the one shown in **figure 58.**

figure 58

2 Cards and decorations

Interlocking skyscraper

This interlocking skyscraper will make an unusual decoration for your party.

Take a sheet of paper, fold it in half and then open it out again, as shown in **figure 59**. Fold the outer edges in to meet the centre crease as in **figure 60**. Next fold the

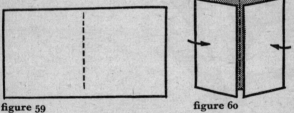

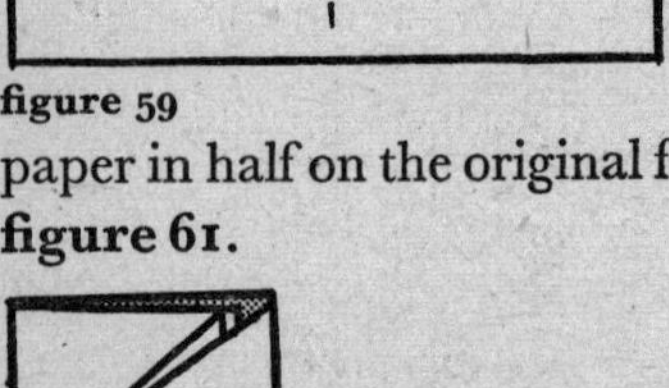

figure 59

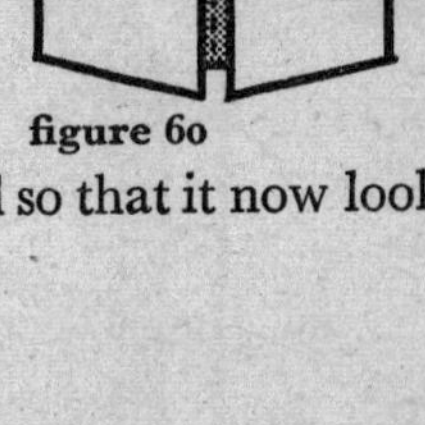

figure 60

paper in half on the original fold so that it now looks like **figure 61**.

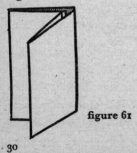

figure 61

Using a pair of scissors, make several cuts to within
1 cm of the centre fold as shown in **figure 62**. Open out

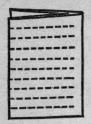

figure 62

the paper very carefully and then fold alternate strips
backwards and forwards. The only point to be careful
with here is that if the top strip of the left-hand section
is folded forwards, then the top strip of the right-hand
section must be folded backwards, and vice versa. Your
paper should now look like **figure 63**.

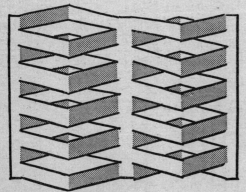

figure 63

Very carefully fold along the centre crease so that the
points of the two halves interlock and your completed
sculpture looks like **figure 64**. Several of these made in

different colours and hung
by thread around the
room will make an
interesting addition to
your party decorations.

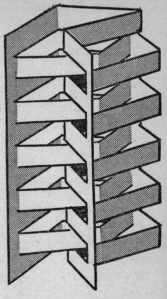

figure 64

String of diamonds

Take a long strip of paper about 7 cm wide and fold it,
concertina fashion, as in **figure 65**. Draw on the front
of the paper the patterns shown in **figure 66** and, with

figure 65

figure 66

a pair of scissors, cut along the lines you have drawn, cutting through all the layers of paper at the same time. When you open out the paper you will have a string of diamonds like that in **figure 67**.

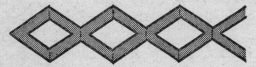

figure 67

If you make a number of these strings, using paper of different colours, you can glue them together to make a long chain of many colours that you can hang up as a pretty decoration for your party.

If you want to be a little more adventurous try cutting out some of the designs shown in **figures 68, 69, 70,** and see what sort of chains they produce. When you have done this, why not think up some designs of your own?

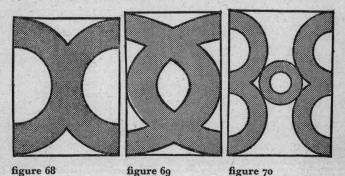

figure 68   figure 69   figure 70

Paper chains

To make paper chains you will need three or four sheets of paper, each sheet being a different colour, a pair of scissors, and some glue.

Place a sheet of newspaper, or a cloth, on the table before you start – just in case you make a mess. Cut each sheet into strips about 2 cm wide by 8 cm long.

Take one strip and glue the ends together to make it into a loop. Pick up a strip of a different colour and thread it through the first loop before sticking the ends together so that you now have two loops joined together. Continue the chain in the same way, as shown in **figure 71,** varying the colours of the strips that you use

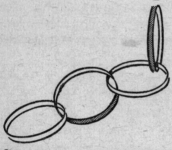

figure 71

until you have a chain of the length that you need for your party decoration, as in **figure 72.**

figure 72

With a bit of imagination you will find that you can think up some ways to make your decorations a little bit different from everyone else's. Some ideas are shown in **figures 73** and **74**.

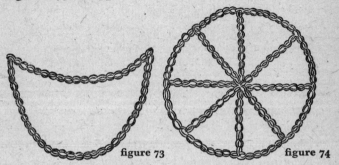

figure 73   figure 74

Frilly chains

Paper chains such as those just described can be made much more attractive if you cut patterns out of the paper strips first. Here are some ways of doing this, but with a little thought you should be able to discover many more.

Fold each strip in half and then draw a pattern on it like that shown in **figure 75**. Cut out the pattern and then,

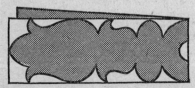

figure 75

when you have several cut-out strips in an assortment of colours, link the strips together in chains as in **figure 76**.

Another way to make the pattern is to fold the strip lengthways before cutting out the design. Or fold it concertina fashion. The variety of the designs that you can make is limited only by your own imagination and patience.

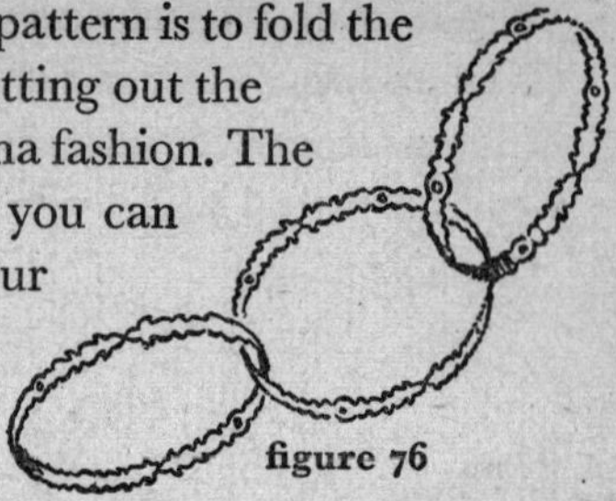

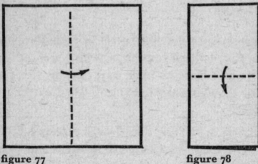

figure 76

Christmas star

To make a star for your Christmas tree you will need a square of paper, folded into quarters as shown in **figures 77** and **78**. Now fold it in half diagonally as in

figure 77

figure 78

figure 79, so that you have a triangular-shaped paper

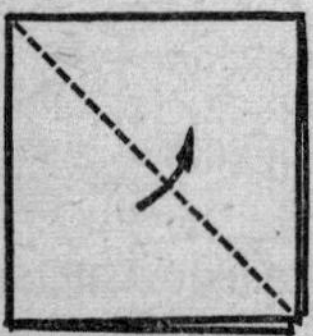

figure 79

(figure 80). With a pair of scissors cut along the dotted lines shown in **figure 80**, and when you open out the

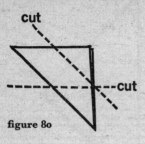

figure 80

paper you will have a beautiful eight-pointed star, as in **figure 81**. It is a good idea to use silver foil or coloured paper to make this star.

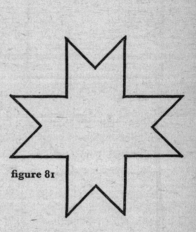

figure 81

Another Christmas star

Here, in **figure 82**, is another star you can make for your Christmas decorations. Take a square sheet of paper and fold it, diagonally, in half. Fold it in half again; and then in half again.

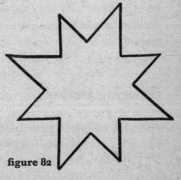

figure 82

These folds are shown in **figures 83** to **86**.

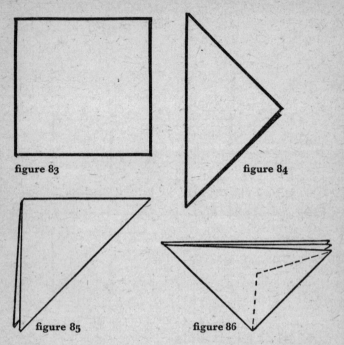

figure 83

figure 84

figure 85

figure 86

Cut along the dotted lines shown in **figure 86**, and open out the paper. By varying the size and shape of this triangular cut you can make several different types of star.

Hanging baskets

Made in coloured paper, these hanging baskets will provide an attractive decoration for your party.

Take a sheet of paper about 14 cm square, fold it in half diagonally, and in half again. With a pair of scissors cut parallel slits in the paper as shown in **figure 87**, cutting almost to the opposite edge.

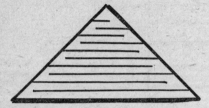

figure 87

Now open the paper out very carefully and it will look like **figure 88**.

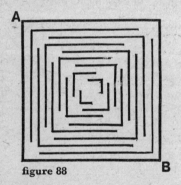

figure 88

Pick up the sheet by the two opposite corners, A and B (**figure 88**), give the paper a shake and you have a pretty basket, like the one in **figure 89**, that you hang up by the two corners.

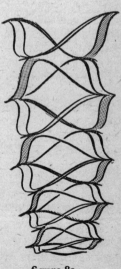

figure 89

Serviette shape

A nice touch in your party decorations is to have the serviettes used for the meal folded in a decorative way.

First fold each into three (**figure 90**). Next fold the right end over to the centre as in **figure 91** and the left end in

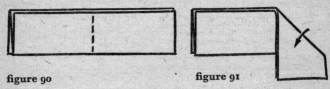

figure 90   figure 91

to meet it, **figure 92**. The bottom ends are now folded up (**figure 93**) and the shape is completed by inserting the bottom corners, one inside the other, as in **figure 94**.

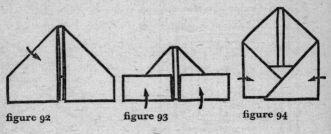

figure 92   figure 93   figure 94

Mitred serviette

Here is another way of folding a serviette to make an attractive table decoration. This one is quite complicated, so follow each move carefully.

Fold up one-third of the serviette, as in **figure 95**. Fold down the top third, placing it between the two lower layers (**figure 96**). Next, fold the two ends into the

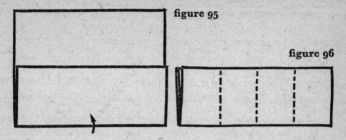

figure 95

figure 96

centre as shown in **figure 97** and turn the top right corner and the lower left corner to the centre as in **figure 98**; then turn the serviette over, **figure 99,**

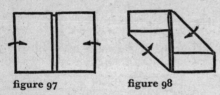

figure 97

figure 98

and fold towards you along the dotted line. Lift up the right-hand flap, **figure 100**, and then turn the packet

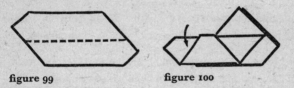

figure 99

figure 100

over and do the same on the other side, **figure 101.**

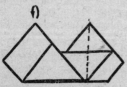

figure 101

Fold towards you along the dotted line in **figure 101** and tuck the corner in, **figure 102**. Turn the serviette over and do the same on the other side, **figure 103**. All

figure 102

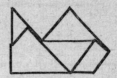

figure 103

you now have to do is to push your finger into the bottom, to make your mitred serviette into a pleasing rounded shape, **figure 104**.

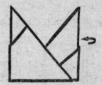

figure 104

Christmas tree card

Here's a Christmas card that is very easy to make. All you need is a piece of thin white card about 15 cm long and 12 cm wide.

Fold it in half lengthways. To make a good, permanent fold, run your ruler down the edge of the card.

Now draw half a Christmas tree on the card as shown in **figure 105**. Do not forget to put a base at the bottom of the card or it will tend to fall over.

Cut out the shape, draw some decorations and the words 'Happy Christmas' on the front of the tree and leave the inside white so that you can write in who it is from (**figure 106**).

figure 105

figure 106

Some other designs are given in **figures 107** and **108**.

figure 107

figure 108

Another hanging basket

Fold a square of paper as shown in **figures 109** to **112**.

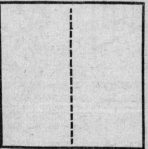

figure 109

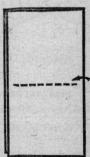

figure 110

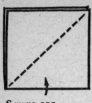

figure 111

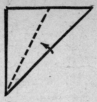

figure 112

Now fold the resultant triangle of paper in half (**figure 113**) and cut off the odd piece of paper, so that you now

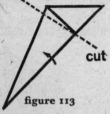

cut

figure 113

have a shape like that in **figure 114**. Cut several slits up and down the triangle, **figure 114**, open out the paper,

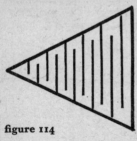

figure 114

and you have another basket for your party decorations, **figure 115**.

figure 115

Seeing stars

Here is yet another way of making stars for your party decorations but this time you can make two stars at the same time; a small star, and a large star with a star-shaped hole in the middle.

Take a square of paper and fold it into quarters. Now fold it in half diagonally and then open it out again (**figure 116**), the purpose being simply to make a crease

figure 116

across the centre of the paper. Fold one edge in to meet the crease and then fold the paper over twice more as shown in **figures 117** and **117a**.

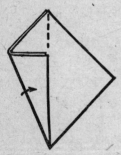

figure 117

figure 117a

Make two diagonal cuts as shown by the dotted lines in **figure 118**. The small bottom portion will be star-shaped; the main centre portion is a star with a star-shaped hole in the middle; and, if you want it, the top portion is a square with a large star-shaped hole in it!

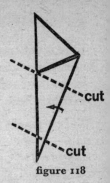

figure 118

Birthday cards

Birthday cards can be made in the same way as the Christmas tree card described on page 42, simply by selecting an appropriate design and drawing it on the card before cutting out.

To make a card in the shape of the person's age you follow the same principle. Some suggestions are given in the illustrations (**figures 119, 120, 121**). The only thing to be careful of when designing these cards is that you do not make too many cuts along the centre fold or

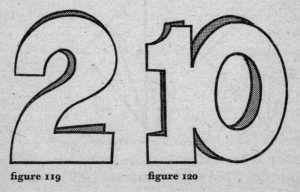

figure 119   figure 120

the card may just fall to pieces instead of opening out properly! It is a good idea to make one in paper first, before making the card.

A star in one

figure 121

Here is an easy way to make a cut-out star that does not require any complicated measuring and which is made using only one cut with a pair of scissors.

This is how you do it: Take a square sheet of paper and fold it in half, **figure 122**. Now follow the folds shown in

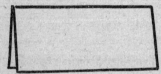

figure 122

figures 123, 124, 125. First fold the paper slanting to the left (**figure 123**), then to the right (**figure 124**) and finally in half so that the folded paper now looks like

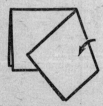

figure 123

figure 124

47

that in **figure 125**. Cut along the dotted line in **figure 125**, open out the upper, triangular piece of paper, and you have a five-pointed star, as in **figure 126**.

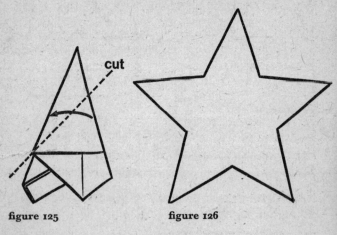

figure 125

figure 126

Pop-up card

To make a pop-up card you will need a piece of thin card about 15 cm by 30 cm.

Fold the card in half length-ways and place it on the table so that the folded edge is on the right. Bring the top right corner down until it meets the left-hand edge and use the edge of a ruler to make a definite crease, **figure 127**.

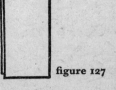

figure 127

Open out the card and fold it in half the other way as in **figure 128**. The creased section of the card should be facing you. Fold the card from left to right and pull the V-crease down into the centre of the fold, **figure 129**.

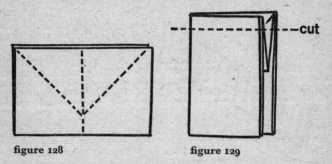

figure 128   figure 129

Next cut off about 4 cm from the top of the card (along the dotted line in **figure 129**). Open out the card and the centre portion will pop up. Draw an appropriate design on this pop-up portion and cut around the top where it extends over the top of the card, so that it now looks like **figure 130**. Decorate your card with paints or crayons, write your greetings and the card is complete.

figure 130

Christmas chain

Take a strip of coloured paper and fold it in half
lengthways. Now cut slits in the paper alternately from
top and bottom as shown in **figure 131**. Open out the

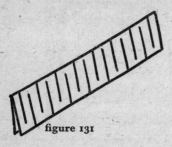

figure 131

paper and you have a decorative Christmas chain
(**figure 132**) which, if joined to similar chains of
different colours, will make a nice display for the
festivities.

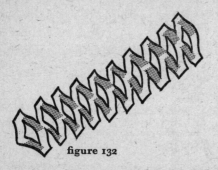

figure 132

If you fold the strip of paper into four, concertina
fashion (**figure 133**) and then make the same cuts, you
will end up with a double chain like that shown in
figure 134.

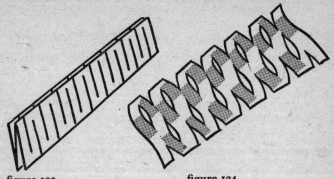

figure 133   figure 134

Another alternative is to fold the strip in half lengthways as for the first chain, then fold it in half again. Make the cuts as before and you will have a triple chain that looks extremely attractive (**figure 135**).

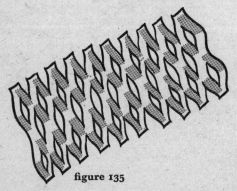

figure 135

Try some other ways of folding the paper, or vary the way it is cut, and see what results you get. But do not waste your coloured paper for this. Use newspapers, then when you find a pattern you like you can make chains of your own design.

Silver snowflake

This decoration is best made out of silver paper but it can of course be made from any paper, then painted an appropriate colour.

Cut out a circle about the size of a 10p piece and then make eight slits in it as in **figure 136**. Give the outer edge of each section a twist and you will end up with the snowflake shape shown in **figure 137**. Several of these, strung together with cotton, will make a colourful addition to your party decorations.

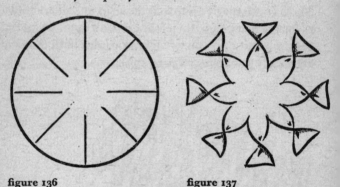

figure 136   figure 137

Magic lanterns

Take a piece of coloured paper about 15 cm by 21 cm. Fold it in half lengthways and then, from the fold to about 2 cm from the top, make a number of cuts, each about 1 cm apart, as in **figure 138**.

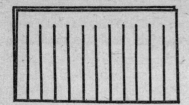

figure 138

Open out the paper and glue the ends together to make the body of the lantern as shown in **figure 139**. A strip of paper stuck over the top makes a neat handle.

The lantern is very attractive as it is, but can be made more so by taking a sheet of paper the same size as the first but of a contrasting colour, rolling it into a tube and sticking it into the centre of the lantern, as in **figure 140**.

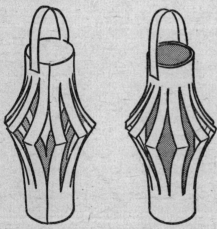

figure 139   **figure 140**

Coloured cellophane looks extremely effective if used for the centre tube.

It is possible to put Christmas tree lights into these lanterns but do not use anything stronger as they may burn the paper. In any case you should get an adult to do this for you.

Paper baubles

Attractive baubles can be made for your Christmas tree with just a few sheets of thin card or coloured paper as follows.

Draw **figure 141** on a sheet of coloured paper.

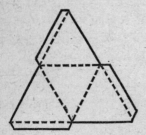

figure 141

Cut along the black lines and fold inwards on the dotted lines. Place a small spot of glue on each of the tabs and then glue the figure together so that you have a pyramid like that shown in **figure 142**.

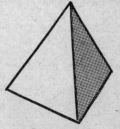

figure 142

Some other shapes are shown in **figures 143 to 146.**

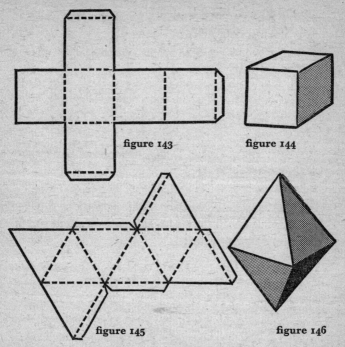

figure 143

figure 144

figure 145

figure 146

Further shapes can be made by gluing together some of these figures. The shape in **figure 147**, for example, is constructed out of five pyramids glued together.

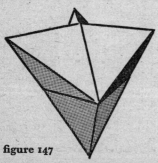

figure 147

That in **figure 148** is simply
three cubes of different
size.

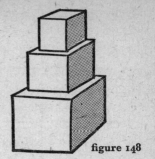

figure 148

Interlocking ball

These interlocking balls are a little complicated to make
but are well worth the effort, especially if made out of
different colours of card.

You will need three circles of card, each the same size.
Cut slits in each of the circles A, B, and C as shown in
figure 149.

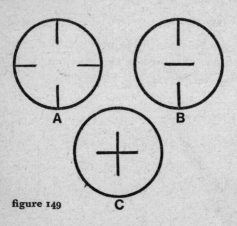

figure 149

Now fold circle A in half and push it, for half of its length, through the centre of circle B. It should now be possible to open circle A out once again.

Next fold circles A and B together and push them through the centre of circle C. Open them out carefully and you will have an interlocking ball like that shown in **figure 150**. A length of cotton, for hanging the ball up, completes the job.

figure 150

3 Puzzles

Letter transformation

Cut out the letter N from a postcard. It is possible, by cutting, to change this N into an M. How can this be done and what is the smallest number of cuts that have to be made? See **figure 151**.

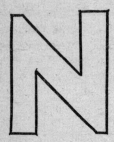

figure 151

You will find the solution to this puzzle on page 64.

T-time test

Copy the four shapes in **figure 152** on to a piece of paper or card. Cut them out and try to arrange them into the shape of the letter T. *Solution, page 64.*

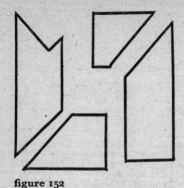

figure 152

A quarter of three-quarters

Take a square piece of paper. Fold it in half and then in half again. Open it out and cut out one of the quarters indicated by the folds so that the piece of paper is now the shape shown in **figure 153**.

figure 153

Now see if you can divide the shape into four equal parts, each part being of the same shape. *Solution, page 65.*

Catching a lion

Trace **figure 154** on to a postcard and then challenge your friends to get the lion into the cage without bending, cutting, or tearing the paper. *Solution, page 65.*

figure 154

It's a date

Challenge your friends to write down any year, for example 1576, without taking their pencil from the paper.

Can you do it? *Solution, page 66.*

Five to one

On a sheet of paper draw a figure consisting of five squares, as in **figure 155**. Having done this, cut out the complete L-shape.

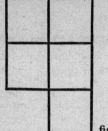

figure 155

The problem is now to make two cuts in the paper and then to rearrange the pieces so that they form one large square. *Solution, page 66.*

Five squared

Copy the five shapes in **figure 156** on to a piece of card and cut them out.

Now see if
you can form
them into a
square.
Solution, page 67.

figure 156

The cross and squares

Draw a cross, like that shown in **figure 157**, on a piece of card and then cut it out.

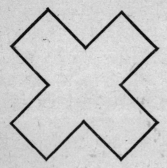

figure 157

Now, see if you can cut it into five pieces which, when rearranged, will form two separate squares, one of which is to have an area exactly half the area of one of the arms of the cross. *Solution, page 67.*

Getting cross

From a sheet of card cut out four Z shapes, all the same size, like that shown in **figure 158**.

Now try to place the four pieces together so that they form a cross. None of the pieces must overlap any of the others. *Solution, page 68.*

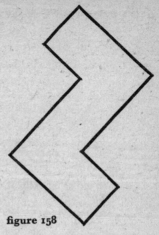

figure 158

4 Answers to puzzles

These answers are the solutions to the puzzles on pages 58 to 63.

Letter transformation

In fact, only one cut need be made to change the letter N into an M. **Figure 159** shows how the letter N is cut and **figure 160** shows how the two pieces are rejoined to form the letter M.

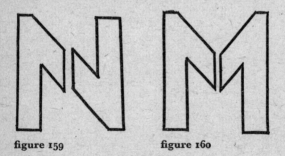

figure 159   figure 160

T-time test

Arrange the four pieces as shown in **figure 161**.

figure 161

A quarter of three-quarters

Divide the shape as shown in **figure 162**.

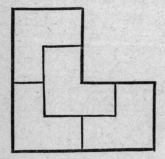

figure 162

Catching a lion

This is in fact a famous optical illusion. To get the lion into the cage, hold the card up in front of you and keep your eyes on the central, dotted line, as you bring the card closer to your face. The lion will appear to go into the cage.

It's a date

This is quite simple when you know how. Simply fold down the top of the paper and write the date as shown in **figure 163**. Unfold the paper and the selected number is clearly visible.

figure 163

Five to one

To make a square from the L–shaped piece of paper, make two cuts as shown in **figure 164**, and rearrange the pieces as in **figure 165**.

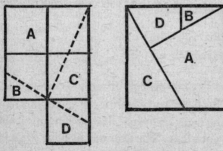

figure 164

figure 165

Five squared

Arrange the pieces as shown in **figure 166**.

figure 166

The cross and squares

Cut the cross as in **figure 167**. Section E itself forms a

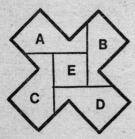

figure 167

square and the four remaining pieces are rearranged as in **figure 168**.

figure 168

Getting cross

The four Z shapes are placed together as shown in
figure 169.

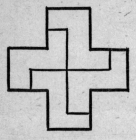

figure 169

5 Puzzling tricks

Puzzling shapes

To make this puzzle you will need three postcards.

Cut the first postcard into an oblong, **figure 170**, the

figure 170

second into two joined triangles, **figure 171**, and the
third into a circle, **figure 172**.

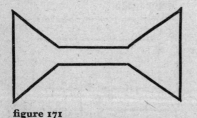

figure 171

figure 172

Bend the oblong over at the centre and place the circle
over it as in **figure 173**. (Try not to crease the oblong as

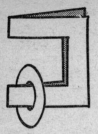

figure 173

this may provide a clue to your unfortunate friend who is going to try to solve the puzzle later.) Fold the two triangles and place them over *one* bar of the oblong as in **figure 174**. Place the circle over the top of the triangles as in **figure 175**. Then open out the oblong so that the

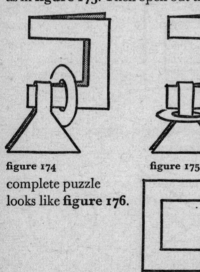

figure 174

complete puzzle
looks like **figure 176**.

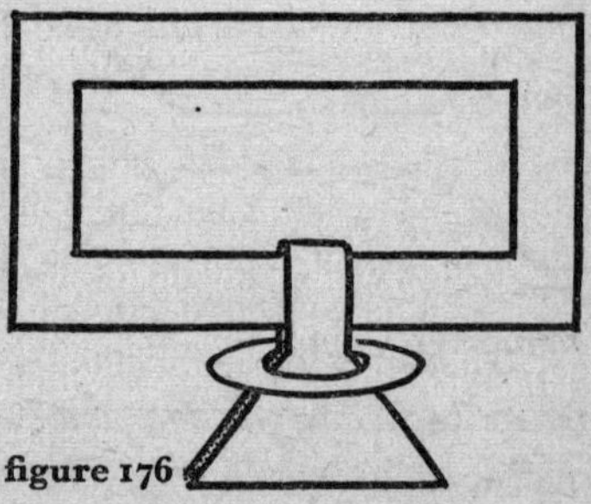

figure 175

figure 176

Ask a friend if he can remove the triangles without tearing anything. If he has not read this book it is going to take him a long, long time to find the answer!

You, of course, can easily remove the triangle by doing the above moves in reverse order, starting with the final move, and working back to the first one.

Chain of mystery

Your party guests will be truly puzzled by this decoration when you point it out to them. It is a chain made of coloured cardboard links, **figure 177**. There appears to be nothing remarkable about it until it is pointed out that not one of the links has a join in it and it is, in fact, made from a single sheet of card. They will never be able to work out how it was made.

figure 177

The secret can be seen in **figure 178**. This shape is first drawn on cardboard and then cut out; but where the black dashes are shown in the centre portions the

figure 178

71

cardboard is scored with a penknife. This scoring must go only half-way through the surface of the card. The dotted lines show where to score on the other side of the cardboard. Once again it is important that the scoring goes only half-way through the cardboard. The card is then peeled apart at these points and the completed links will then form as shown. If the chain is then painted, areas where the cardboard is only half of its original thickness will not be noticeable.

That's torn it!

If you like playing jokes on your friends then try this one.

Bet a friend that he cannot touch his toes. As he bends down to prove you wrong, tear a strip of paper that you have concealed behind your back. The ripping sound will make your friend think that he has torn his trousers!

Button release

To prepare for this trick, make two cuts in a postcard, each about 6 cm long and 1 cm apart. Just below the cuts make a small hole about 1 cm in diameter. Thread a length of cotton through the cuts and through the hole and tie a button to each end of the cotton, as shown in **figure 179**. Thus prepared, the card can be carried in your pocket until you want to perform the trick.

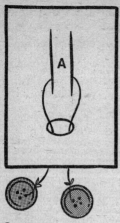

figure 179

Challenge a friend to remove the cotton and buttons from the card without tearing the card or breaking the thread. He will not be able to do it but you can, as follows: fold the card forwards, and push the cut-out strip (A) through the hole so that it forms a loop on the other side of the card. Push one of the buttons through this loop and when the card is returned to its original position the buttons and thread are free!

Try your strength

This stunt sounds impossible until you try it – and then, when you realize that it does work, it becomes quite a puzzler.

Take an ordinary ruler and place it on the table so that about 5 cm projects over the edge of the table. Take a

73

double sheet from a newspaper and lay it on the table over the ruler. The nearest edge of the paper should be about 3 cm from, and parallel to, the edge of the table (**figure 180**).

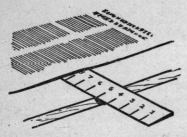

figure 180

Raise your fist above the projecting end of the ruler and bring it down as hard as you can. Much to your surprise you will find that the paper and ruler do not go sailing through the air as you might have expected but lift only a few centimetres from the table.

The ruler must be hit fair and square or the paper may tear. Sometimes the ruler itself will snap! But whatever else may happen the newspaper never flies up in the air.

Try this on your friends as a test of strength. Challenge them to knock the paper in the air simply by banging the ruler and they will be astonished to find out how weak they really are. In actual fact, this amazing stunt has nothing to do with strength but is due to the pressure on the ruler that is exerted by the paper.

Blow a little harder

Here is another test of strength that you can try on your friends.

Take an ordinary postcard and bend each end down, about 1 cm from the edge, and place the card on a table as shown in **figure 181**.

Now challenge your friends to blow the card over. Try as hard as they may, they will not be able to do it!

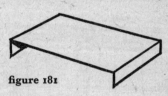

figure 181

Powerful paper

For this trick you need a piece of paper – 8 cm by 14 cm is about the right size – and a beaker.

Challenge your friends to balance the beaker on the paper. After scratching their heads for a while they will eventually give up. You then show them how to do it.

Fold the paper into five equal portions and stand it on the table. Then gently place the beaker across the fold in the centre and it will balance on the paper as shown in **figure 182**.

figure 182

Linking clips

This is a neat and puzzling trick. You may even baffle yourself with this one!

Take a piece of paper and fold it into the shape of the letter S. Place two paper-clips on the paper, in the positions shown in **figure 183**.

figure 183

Now pull each end of the paper sharply apart. The two clips will jump off the paper, giving everyone quite a surprise.

But an even bigger surprise is to come, for when the clips are picked up they are found to be linked together!

Odd or even

The numbers from 1 to 9 are written on a postcard which is then torn into nine pieces, and the pieces are dropped into a box or a hat. After the pieces are mixed up in the box you, though blindfold, are able to pick out any piece and tell if the number on it is odd or even.

The secret of this trick depends upon the way that the numbers are written down and the fact that the card is torn, not cut. If you look at **figure 184**, you will see that the even numbers have only one straight edge to them, but that all the odd numbers have two straight edges, with the exception of number 5 which has none. It is, therefore, an easy matter to feel the edges of each piece of card before bringing it into view and you know instantly whether it is odd or even.

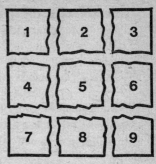

figure 184

The disappearing square

Here is a puzzling trick that you can show to your friends. Draw **figure 185** on a piece of paper. Each square should be the same size, say 1.5 cm, and the drawing must be 13 squares by 5 – a total of 65 squares.

Cut the card into four pieces as shown in **figure 185** and reassemble them as in **figure 186**.

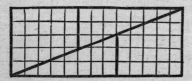

figure 185

figure 186

If you now count the squares you will find that there are only 64 – one square has mysteriously disappeared!

Walking through paper

Taking a sheet of paper about 20 cm square, you tell your friends that you can cut a hole in the paper large enough for you to walk through, and this you proceed to do.

This is how you do it. Fold the paper into half and then into quarters, as in **figure 187**. With a pair of scissors

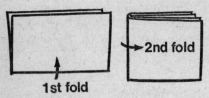

1st fold   2nd fold

figure 187

cut along the fold, from the bottom to within 2 cm of the top edge (**figure 188**). Now make alternate horizontal cuts from the left and right edges, as shown in **figure 189**. Stop about 2 cm from the edge of the paper in each case. Open out the paper, being careful not to tear it in

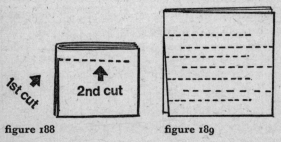

1st cut   2nd cut

figure 188   **figure 189**

the process, and you will have a loop that is large enough to go over your body (**figure 190**).

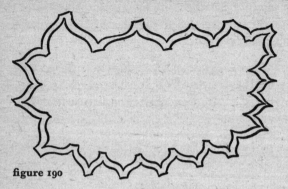

figure 190

(Another method of cutting the paper to achieve this intriguing effect can be found in my book *Amaze and Amuse Your Friends*.)

That's the name

This trick gives people the impression that you are a real mind-reader. Although simple to do, it is, nevertheless, extremely effective.

You will need about nine or ten slips of paper measuring approximately 10 cm by 2 cm, a pencil, an ash-tray, and a box of matches.

Ask someone to call out the name of a famous person. This you write on the first slip, then fold the slip in half and drop it in the ash-tray. Other names are called out and they in turn are each written on a slip, which is folded, and dropped into the ash-tray. When all the slips are completed you mix them up a little and then ask someone to pick out any one. The rest are burnt and, gazing intently into the flames, you tell the audience the name on the selected slip. When this is opened it is seen that you are correct.

How is it done? Simple. All you do is to write the first name on every slip. As all the slips therefore bear the same name, the trick is incredibly easy to do and the burning of the unselected slips, in addition to adding to the air of mystery, destroys all the evidence as to how you achieved this mind-reading miracle.

The Afghan bands

This is a really astonishing trick but one that is quite easy to make, and even easier to perform.

You will need three long bands of paper, each about 1 metre long by 8 cm wide.

Take the first strip and glue the ends together so that it forms a continuous loop as in **figure 191**. Do the same

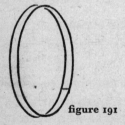

figure 191

with the second strip but give one end of it one complete turn before joining the ends. With the third strip, give one end two turns before the loop is joined. You are now ready to perform.

If the first band is cut down the centre you will get two narrow bands as one would expect, **figure 192**. When

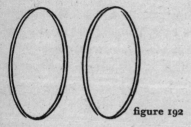

figure 192

the second band is cut down the centre there are again two bands – but they are linked together, as in **figure 193**. The third band is even more surprising, for, when it is cut down the middle, it produces not two bands but one – twice the size of the others! (See **figure 194**.)

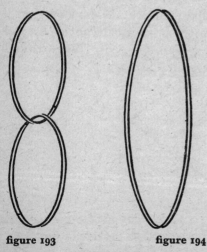

figure 193   figure 194

Sawing a lady in half

One of the best-known tricks performed by magicians is that of sawing a lady in half. Here is a version of this famous trick that you can perform for your friends.

You will need a long envelope, in the back of which are two secret cuts (**figure 195**). You will also need a cut-out cardboard picture of a lady, and a pair of scissors. The cuts need to be a little wider than the widest part of the lady.

figure 195

Show the lady to your audience and also show them the envelope (**figure 195**) – but do not let anyone see the slits in the back. Cut off the two ends of the envelope to make it into a tube, as in **figure 196**.

figure 196

Place the lady into one end of the envelope tube and through the first slit. She is then pushed on, through the second slit, until her feet are showing at one end and her head at the other. It should appear that all you have done is to place her in the tube. **Figure 197** shows what the audience sees and **figure 198** shows your view.

figure 197   **figure 198**

You now cut through the envelope, making sure that the blade of the scissors is *in front of* the lady, as in **figure 198**. It appears that you have cut through the lady as well, but when you pull her out of the envelope she is still in one piece. It must be magic!

6 Toys and games

The flying cross

From a postcard, or sheet of thin card, cut a square with sides measuring 7 cm. From each corner cut a 2.5 cm square so that you now have a cross, **figure 199**.

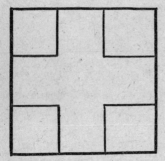

figure 199

Balance the cross on your left fingers with one of its arms extending over your fingers on the right-hand side. Now, with your right hand, flick the projecting arm of the cross. This flick is achieved by pressing the nail of the first finger against the ball of the thumb and then releasing it, sharply. The cross will spin into the air quite dramatically. With a bit of practice you will find that it is possible to make the cross fly in a circle and come back to you like a boomerang.

Jet-propelled boat

To make this jet-propelled boat you will need a post-card, a pair of scissors, some soap-powder (detergent), and of course a bowl of water in which to sail it.

Cut out from the postcard the shape of a boat as shown in **figure 200**, and place it gently on the surface

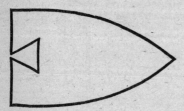

figure 200

of the water. With a spoon or the tip of a knife carefully place a small quantity of detergent into the triangular cut-out and after a few seconds your boat will start to move forwards as if by magic.

Spinning helicopter

Cut a piece of paper to the shape shown in **figure 201**.

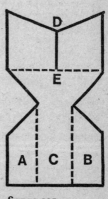

figure 201

Fold the portions A and B on to section C and glue them down or stick a piece of Sellotape on them to hold them together. Cut down the line D–E and fold the two top portions over in opposite directions. Your piece of paper should now look like **figure 202**.

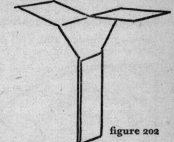

Throw the paper up into the air and it will spin as it returns to the ground.

figure 202

Whizzer wheel

To make this whizzer wheel you will need a sheet of card, a length of string or elastic, and some paints or crayons.

From the card, cut out a circle with a diameter of about 12 cm. Make two holes about 1 cm apart in the centre of the disc, through which the elastic is threaded, as shown in **figure 203**. The two ends of the elastic are tied together to form a continuous loop.

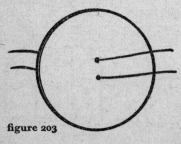

figure 203

Place your hands in each end of the loop and swing the disc round and round, then separate the hands as far as they will go and the disc will spin. As it reaches the end of its spin bring the hands inwards, and the disc will wind itself up again. By alternately tightening and slackening the elastic the disc can be kept spinning for some considerable time.

Why not make several discs and paint patterns on them as shown in **figures 204, 205, 206**?

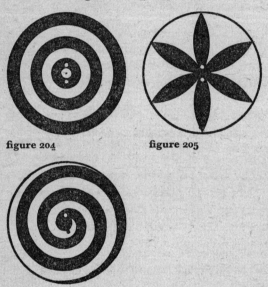

figure 204   figure 205

figure 206

The turning wonder

On a piece of card about the size of a playing-card draw a birdcage, **figure 207**; and on the other side, but

figure 207

figure 208

upside-down, draw a bird, **figure 208**. Now make a hole in the centre of either end of the card and tie a short piece of string in each hole, as in **figure 209**.

figure 209

Twist the string backwards and forwards between the finger and thumb of each hand so that the card begins to revolve.

The bird will appear to be inside the cage.

The official name for this toy is 'thaumatrope' which comes from the Greek words for 'turning wonder'.

Revolving snake

Cut a large circle out of a piece of thick paper or thin card and draw a spiral on it, as in **figure 210**. Cut along the line you have drawn.

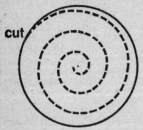

figure 210

Now balance what was the centre of the circle on a knitting-needle or a pencil, **figure 211**, and hold it near a draught or some heat. The snake will revolve as though alive.

You could make several of these snakes and hang them on a mobile as shown in **figure 212**. Painted in striking colours they make a fascinating display.

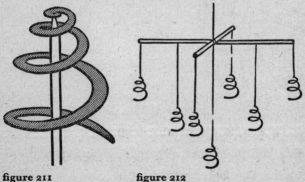

figure 211   **figure 212**

A flying wind wheel

Take a piece of card about 10 cm square and draw on it a large circle. Draw another circle having the same centre, but with a radius 1 cm less than the first. Divide the smaller circle into sixteen sections, as shown in **figure 213**.

figure 213

Now cut out the large circle and also cut along the lines dividing the small circle. Bend these inner segments alternately up and down so that the card now looks like **figure 214**.

figure 214

On a windy day stand the wheel upright and then let it go. The wind will roll it away at an amazing rate and you may have quite a job catching it!

The interlocking ball described on page 56 makes another excellent wind toy.

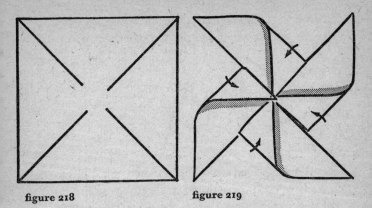

figure 218   **figure 219**

Paper parachute

To make a paper parachute, all you need is a square of paper (strong tissue paper is best), a toy soldier, scissors, a needle, and some cotton.

Fold the paper as shown in **figures 220, 221**. It is first folded into quarters and then folded diagonally in half.

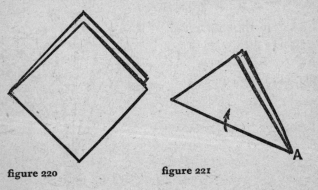

figure 220   **figure 221**

With the scissors trim off the corner A as shown in **figure 222**. When the paper is opened out you will have

figure 222

a scalloped-edged circle, **figure 223**, to which several lengths of cotton are then attached. Be careful that you do not tear the paper when you attach the cotton.

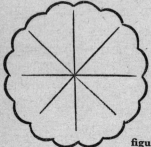

figure 223

Finally tie the ends of the cotton to the toy soldier, **figure 224**, and your parachute is complete.

figure 224

Right on target

Here is a game that is simple to make; all you need is a sheet of paper, three or four coloured pencils, and a few buttons.

Draw a large circle on the paper and draw four more circles inside it, as in **figure 225**. There is no need for

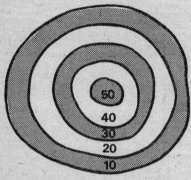

figure 225

these circles to be perfect. In fact, it may make the game harder and more interesting if they are definitely not circular. If you look at **figure 226**, you will see that there are several designs for this target. Colour the various rings or target areas and give each a numerical value.

The target is placed on the floor a short distance away and the players then take turns to flip or throw the buttons on to it. The button must be definitely in an area to score the appropriate number of points. If the button is touching a line then it scores nothing. Total up

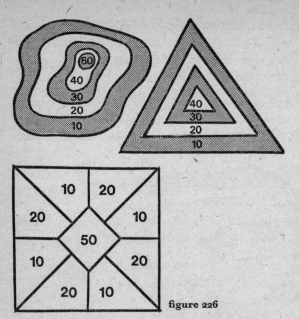

figure 226

each player's score and the first person to reach 100 is the winner.

Flying fish race

Here is a great game that requires only a few pieces of paper, some books, and a piece of string.

Cut fish shapes out of the paper, all the fish being of the same shape and size. Using a felt-tipped pen, mark each fish with a number so that it is easily identifiable.

Place the fish in a row on the floor at the far end of the room; lay down the string to mark the winning post.

Each player is given a book. This is to be waved up and down behind a fish, the wind set up by the book causing the fish to jump up and forwards. The first fish past the line is, of course, the winner.

The fish must be moved only by the book being waved up and down; the book must not touch the fish; and interference with another player's fish is not permitted.

What's my name?

For this game you will need several postcards, a ball of string, a pair of scissors, and a pencil or felt-tipped pen.

With the scissors make a small hole in one end of each postcard and thread the card on to a length of string. Tie the ends of the string together to form a loop large enough to go over a person's head without difficulty.

On each card write the name of some famous character of fact or fiction. For example, you could write Robinson Crusoe on one card, Queen Elizabeth I on another, and so on.

Each player has one of these labels on his back, held there by the loop of string placed over his head. Each individual must then ask questions of the others such as 'Am I male?', 'Am I a fictional character?', etc. and the first person to guess who he or she is wins the game. All questions must be answered truthfully by the other players but they are allowed to give only a simple 'yes' or 'no' answer.

Boxes

Here is another game for two people that requires only a pencil and a sheet of paper.

Draw on the paper ten lines of evenly spaced dots, as in **figure 227**. The two players now take it in turns to draw a line, either horizontal or vertical, to connect two dots. The person who draws the line that completes a square writes his or her initial in the square (see **figure 228**) and the person who wins the highest number of squares is the winner.

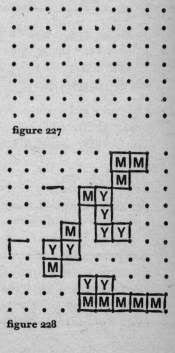

figure 227

The skill in this game comes towards the end as the number of lines that you can draw without giving away a square to your opponent grow gradually fewer and fewer.

figure 228

Cup and ball

To make this game you will need an empty yoghurt carton, a ping-pong ball or a ball made from paper, and a piece of string.

Make a small hole in the side of the carton and one through the ball. Thread the string through the ball and tie a knot in the end of the string. Do the same with the carton so that the ball is now connected to it by a length of string, as shown in **figure 229**.

figure 229

Swing the ball on the string and try to catch it in the cup. Have a game with a friend – the first one to catch the ball in the cup ten times is the winner.

Ten-pin marbles

Take a shoe box and cut a number of squares out of one edge, as shown in **figure 230**. With a felt-tipped pen write numbers over the top of each hole.

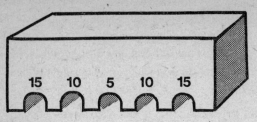

figure 230

The box is placed on the floor and players take it in turns to roll marbles at the holes. Points are scored according to which hole the marble goes through and the first person to reach 100 (or any other number you have decided on), is the winner.

Pass the parcel

This is an extremely popular game for parties. Get a small present and wrap it up in a sheet of paper. Tie the parcel loosely with string or Sellotape. Now wrap the parcel up in another sheet of paper, again tying it loosely. Continue doing this until you have quite a large package. It is a good idea to use different types of paper for each layer, as this makes the game a little more exciting.

Arrange your guests in a circle and hand the parcel to one of them. Switch on your radio to some music. While the music is playing the players are to pass the parcel from one to another. As soon as the person with the radio switches it off, the person holding the parcel at that moment must start to undo the parcel as fast as he or she can.

As soon as the music is switched on again, the person holding the parcel must stop undoing it and it is passed around the circle once more. This continues until the present is finally reached and the one who gets it wins the game, of course.

To be fair, the person switching the radio on and off should be sitting with his back to the players, so that he does not know who has the parcel at any time.

Noughts and crosses

This is an extremely well-known game that is also called Tic, Tac, Toe. All you need to play the game is a sheet of paper, a pencil, and an opponent.

Draw a diagram of nine squares as shown in **figure 231** and you are ready to start.

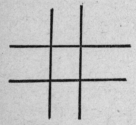

figure 231

The first player marks an X in any one of the nine squares. Then the other player places an O in any square. The players continue to take turns in this way, the object being to achieve a line of three Xs or Os. The first person to get three letters in a row is the winner.

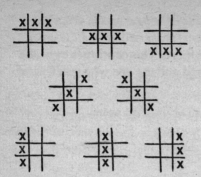

figure 232

There are in fact eight possible winning lines, as can be seen in **figure 232**, but of course each player, in addition to trying to win, also tries to prevent his opponent from doing so.

The donkey's tail

With a felt-tipped pen draw the outline of a donkey on **a** large sheet of brown paper, as in **figure 233**.

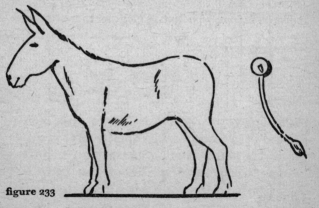

figure 233

Do not give the donkey a tail.

Draw a tail on a sheet of cardboard or an old cereal packet, and cut it out. (Also shown in **figure 233**.)

Place a drawing-pin in the top of the tail and hang the donkey drawing on the wall. Players are blindfolded in turn and given the tail, which they must try to pin in the appropriate place on the drawing. The person who gets the tail nearest to the correct spot is the winner.

Hangman

One player thinks of a word of not more than eight letters and marks a piece of paper with a number of dashes in accordance with the number of letters in the word. Thus, if the word is 'Piccolo', there will be seven dashes. The other player then calls out a letter of the alphabet. If that letter appears in the selected word it is written in above the appropriate dash. For each time the person calls a letter that does not appear in the word draw one part of a picture of a man on the gallows as shown in **figure 234**. The player can therefore have

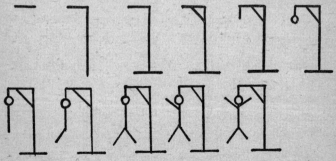

figure 234

eleven incorrect calls before he gets hanged. If this happens, then the person doing the drawing gets a point. If, however, the guesser completes the word successfully, then he gets a point. The first person to reach the number of points you've decided on beforehand is the winner.

The advertisement game

Cut out a number of advertisements from a variety of newspapers and magazines. Cut off all the references to the names of the products advertised and stick the advertisements on to a large board or sheet of card.

When the time comes for the party games, challenge your guests to name the products on the advertisements. The person who gets the highest number correct is, of course, the winner.

Number top

This little top comes in handy for board games when you haven't any dice.

On a piece of thin card draw a small circle about the size of a 10p coin. In fact, an easy way to draw this circle is to place a 10p coin on the card and then run the pencil round its edge. Divide the circle into six sections, number each one from one to six, and then cut out the circle.

Take a match-stick, one end of which is sharpened to a point, and push it through the centre of the circle. You may find this easier to do if you first make a hole in the circle with a pin.

To use the number top it is spun on the table and when it comes to rest, as in **figure 235**, the number nearest the table is the number selected. Sometimes the top will come to rest between numbers, so to avoid confusion it is a good idea to cut the circle into the shape of a hexagon, as shown in **figure 236**.

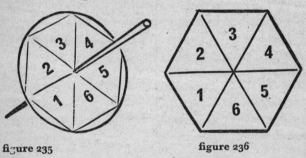

figure 235   figure 236

Battleships

This is a very popular game for two people. All you require are two sheets of paper and two pencils.

Draw a grid of squares on each sheet, number the squares across the top, and letter them a, b, c, d, and so on, down one side. Every square can therefore be known by a number and a letter, 4b, 8f, 7a, etc.

Each player is given a fleet of ships, which he places anywhere on his sheet, in accordance with the following rules: one battleship equals five squares; one cruiser, four squares; two destroyers, three squares; and three submarines, one square each. Each vessel is indicated on the grid by a small cross in the appropriate number of squares. Each vessel of more than one square must, of course, form a straight line. It is, however, permitted to position the vessels diagonally as shown in **figure 237**. Do not show your sheet to your opponent.

	1	2	3	4	5	6	7	8	9	10
a		x	x	x						
b										
c		x	x	x	x	x				
d									x	
e			x						x	
f		x							x	
g	x								x	
h					x					
i			x							
j								x		
k										

figure 237

The two players now take turns to call out a square (using a number and a letter), the object being to sink the enemy fleet. Each time a square is called the other person must say whether or not it has hit a ship and, if it has, must name the type of vessel. As each ship must be a number of squares in a straight line it is an easy matter to sink it in a few goes once its direction has been established. It is a good idea to mark your own paper with a tick in each square called so that you do not fall into the trap of calling the same square twice.

The first player to sink the complete enemy fleet is the winner.

Gone fishing

To make this game you will need some thin card or coloured paper, several paper-clips, Sellotape, and a length of string.

From the paper cut out several fish shapes like that shown in **figure 238**. To each fish you must now affix a

figure 238

paper-clip in the following manner: bend the short arm of the paper-clip upwards as in **figure 239**, and use the Sellotape to stick the long arm of the clip to the paper fish (**figure 240**). Write a number from 1 to 5 on the underside of each fish.

figure 239   figure 240

Bend a paper-clip into a hook and tie one end of the string to it, **figure 241**, like a fishing rod.

figure 241

To play the game, place the fishes on a table, mix them up so that no one knows which is which, and then take it in turns to use the fishing rod to hook the fishes off the table. When all the fishes have been caught, turn them over to see who has got the highest score.

Tailor-made board game

Here is an easy way to make up your own games. All you will need is a large sheet of card or paper, some coloured pencils, some counters or buttons, and the number top described on page 104.

Draw **figure 242** on to the card as large as you can. On the squares marked 'advance' or 'go back', write in an appropriate remark and draw a picture to go with it according to the theme that you have selected for the game.

Here is an example to give you an idea of what you can do:

Let us assume that you decide upon a car race as the theme for your game. You could then fill the 'advance' squares as follows:

1 Good gear change, advance 2 (picture of gear lever)
2 Fast acceleration, advance 3 (picture of car going fast)
3 Downhill section, take extra turn (picture of car going downhill)
4 Short cut, advance 4 (picture of road going over a mountain)

FINISH

START

GO BACK

GO BACK

GO BACK

GO BACK

GO BACK

GO BACK

GO BACK

ADVANCE

ADVANCE

ADVANCE

ADVANCE

figure 242

The 'go back' squares could be:

1 False start, go back 1 (picture of car going backwards)
2 Puncture, go back 2 (picture of flat tyre)
3 Greasy road, go back 3 (picture of skid marks)
4 Run out of petrol, go back 4 (picture of petrol pump)
5 Pit stop, lose turn (picture of car with wheels off)
6 Crash, go back to pit stop (picture of crashed car)
7 Steering fault, go back 4 (picture of steering wheel)

Draw a picture of the winning flag in the large square at the end of the course and the game is ready for playing.

Each player takes it in turn to spin the number top or throw a die and moves his counter along the appropriate number of squares. The first person to reach the flag is the winner.

You could also make your game as a horse-race, a search for buried treasure, or the hunt for a dangerous criminal, or whatever you fancy, but the principles remain the same in each case. You need not, of course, keep to the same layout each time but can vary the shape of the course and alter the number of 'advance' or 'go back' squares as you wish.

Also in Piccolo by Peter Eldin

Amaze and Amuse your Friends! (illus) 25p

With this book you can be an all-round entertainer. It is
packed with interesting and exciting tricks to play on your
friends and family. With a little practice you will have
them gasping with amazement and giggling with
amusement at your truly astonishing conjuring tricks.

There are also hilarious puzzles and (harmless) practical
jokes which are as much fun to do as to watch. The book
has lots of diagrams and cartoons to help you do the tricks.